Lifeless Souls

LIFELESS
SOULS

HOLLY RIORDAN

THOUGHT
CATALOG
Books

BROOKLYN, NY

THOUGHT
CATALOG
Books

Published by Thought Catalog Books, a division of The Thought & Expression Co., Williamsburg, Brooklyn. Founded in 2010, Thought Catalog is a website and imprint dedicated to your ideas and stories. We publish fiction and non-fiction from emerging and established writers across all genres. For general information and submissions: manuscripts@thoughtcatalog.com.

First edition, 2017

ISBN: 978-1945796555

Printed and bound in the United States.

10 9 8 7 6 5 4 3 2 1

CONTENTS

Introduction

For thousands of years, this has been my existence. Listening to stories. Logging those stories. Deciding whether the soul in question gets to experience eternal bliss or is deemed unworthy and is sent to be tortured.

A mortal reveals their ultimate truth when they are faced with death. The rest doesn't matter. Only the end matters.

How did they spend their final moments? Which details do they believe are important enough to mention during their retelling? Do they show remorse? Pride? Hatred? Love? What have they learned from their demise?

Once a soul has ascended to me, I give it a faint touch with the tips of my fingers—that is all it takes to get them to talk, to make them truthful, to make sure the tale they retell is authentic.

Unfortunately, over the course of the last few months, my job has twisted into a new shape. Something has happened. There is a shift on Earth, and the repercussions can be felt here.

I'm afraid of what the next steps may be, of what may happen to me and the kingdom where I dwell, so I have documented the most significant interviews for my successor—or for anyone who is left after the fallout.

1

Adaline DuBois, Age 25

I walked through the door, wrists aching from the weight of six bags of groceries, and found my husband asleep on the couch. My son nowhere to be found. Typical.

I rested the bags on the counter, put away some of the frozen stuff—ice cream and peas and chicken fingers—then moseyed toward Pierre's room to check up on him. I just wanted to give him a kiss. Give myself a reminder of why I worked twelve hour days.

I let myself inside and—Jesus, Mary, and Joseph—the room looked like a shit show. Blocks covering every inch of the floor. Juice stains on his bed sheets. Crayon on the wall.

I'm not proud of myself now that I know the reason he did it, but at the time, I was pissed. Frustrated and tired and pissed. So I bent him over my knee and spanked him. Asked him why the hell he trashed his room.

He sputtered out something about how the robot made him do it. I figured that meant another one of his imaginary friends. He conjured up a donkey once and a duck and maybe a dragon—I can't remember, but he came up with something new all the time. He had an active imagination, the teachers told us that.

He apologized through his snot and tears, so I thought that would be the end of it. He'd always been a good kid. Usually listened. Never caused any trouble.

But during the next few weeks, he came home from school with detention slips. I received phone calls from other parents saying he got into fist fights. Getting him to do homework and go to sleep on time and take a bath became a chore. And, of course, my husband didn't do anything about it so I ended up yelling until my throat turned raw and I looked like the bad guy.

Did you find his change in attitude strange?

It seemed weird, yeah, but I didn't think of it as something supernatural—technological, scientific—whatever the hell you want to call it. I thought he was just acting like a brat. Kids will do that. I went through a phase. Everybody does.

So anyway. One night, I called his name and he refused to answer, which I considered a huge no-no. Being ignored drove me nuts, so I started screaming: *Pierre! Pierre! Goddamn it, Pierre!* I busted into his room and he looked up at me, all confused.

I noticed it right away. No hearing aid in his ear. He left it on his bedside table.

Hearing aid?

Yeah. He popped out of me without any hearing in his left ear and minimal hearing in the right, so he wore a hearing aid at all times. Only took it out for bed when he remembered.

But he wasn't wearing it this time. So I signed to him—we

taught him just enough sign language to get by—and I asked him why he removed it.

He told me he didn't want to hear the voices. He didn't want to hear the robot anymore because it told him to do bad things. All those things that had been getting him into trouble.

I should have…maybe I should have taken him to the doctor right away. But I didn't want him to be afraid of his hearing aid or do something crazy like flush it down the toilet. We paid so much money for that damn thing. So I fed him some bullshit about how safe it was, and, I mean, I put it to my own ear and heard nothing, so I made him stick it back in.

Did the incident occur that day?

No. That happened three days later. I heard him talking inside of his bedroom and thought maybe he'd swiped my cell phone to call a friend. But no, I ended up watching him walking back and forth, having a conversation with himself. Freaking the fuck out. Pulling out hair and banging his fists against the wall. I think I even saw piss stains on his jeans.

Now, most people would say I acted like a shit mother because I didn't go in there and sit down with him and let him cry on my shoulder but, look, I didn't know what the hell to do. I was still in my twenties. Still a clueless kid too stupid to use the pill.

I didn't want to make his meltdown worse, so I left him alone while I flipped through the yellow pages to find the number for a psychiatrist. I thought they would diagnose him with schizophrenia. Some kind of mental disorder. I wanted to get him help.

I got on the phone, listened to it *ring-ring-ring*, and then I realized Pierre had followed me into the kitchen. He held a butcher knife with those little fingers.

I don't know how he snatched it. Maybe he grabbed it while his crackhead father watched him one day and stored it under his pillow until the timing felt right. I really don't know.

All I know is I thought he would hurt himself, that he would slip and jam that thing into his neck.

So I crouched to his level and held out my arms. Cooed to him like a puppy, trying to get him to put down the blade.

Shut up. I don't wanna. Shutupshutupshutup. He kept saying that, over and over again. I thought he was answering me, not the…the voice in his ear. The robot telling him to murder his own mother.

You think that is what the voice said to him?

I mean, I'm here, aren't I?

My son ran into my open arms and as I squeezed him tightly, he stuck the blade deep into my stomach and twisted. After that I bet he did the same thing to his father. The deadbeat was already passed out on the couch. Easy prey. He must have offed him next…

You know, that kid loved me. I may have fucked up at times; I may have actually been a horrible mother, but he loved me.

He didn't kill me.

The AI whispering into his ear did.

2

Cassidy Stevens,
Age 48

A group of us sat outside smoking hash and searching the stars for patterns, right? A helluva lot of UFO activity appeared in that area over the years, so we thought we might spot something that would get our magazine taken seriously. A photograph. A lead of some sort.

And we got what we wanted. A smattering of black dots in the air, almost impossible to see. When I squinted, I could make them out better, could see them zip overhead.

We'd been disappointed too many times before, so my brother waved it off, thinking they looked more like birds. They flew in the same kind of flocking formation. Like they wanted to stick together.

You know what those things turned out to be? Drones.

Harmless—at least that's what I thought until one of them swooped down and snapped a piece of hair off my head. Plucked it with some mechanism that sprouted from the bottom.

The rest of the group, my brother and a few friends from the magazine, said the same damn thing happened to them. They all felt a little pluck.

What did you do?

Went home and wrote up an article that barely got any traffic. That was that.

Except, really, it wasn't at all because I like to stick my nose in places it doesn't belong. I guess that kind of curiosity got me killed.

I waited on that hill again, night after night. Waited for the drones to fly past again. To see if I could learn anything new about them.

After a full month, thirty whole days, they returned, flying the other way around that time.

So I pulled a shotgun from my car, rested it against my shoulder, and shot one of the things out of the sky, first try.

I feel bad about that now, but you have to remember, back then I thought I brought down a machine. Not something…sentient.

But I didn't kill it. I only injured it. Made it sputter to the ground and then grabbed it—and as soon as I wrapped my paws around it, it started blinking with this bright green light.

Now, I taught myself Morse Code back in '99 when I first started looking for flashes in the sky. So I knew what it meant to say.

H – E – L – P

It called for its friends.

And one of them came. Except instead of having a little tweezer-type mechanism attached to pluck out my hair, it held a goddamn grenade.

It hovered there, only a few feet above my head. Maybe it waited as a warning. To give me the chance to escape.

But I didn't let go of its friend, so it let go of its bomb. And *boom*.

Did the drone in your hand get destroyed?

Sure did. I guess it was better for that little fellow to be a casualty, a sacrifice, than for me to take it home to poke and prod at it, to find out something that humans could use to hurt it.

Did you ever find out why it took your DNA?

I suppose for the same reason I wanted to grab the machine and take that home. For research.

Or maybe just plain old curiosity. Maybe they're more like us than we care to admit.

3

Destiny May-Francis, Age 27

I really don't want to talk about it. I'm really not ready to relive it.

I worked with kids. They were my life. As a little girl, I shoved a ball beneath my shirt and held a tree branch like a pregnancy test. I always wanted to carry a baby. Not just have a baby, but carry it.

I wanted strangers at the grocery store to ask me about the gender. I wanted to feel it kick during my drive to work. I wanted the glowing skin and big boobs and even those random food cravings.

But things don't always turn out right, do they?

My husband took me to get an ultrasound on my birthday. I was only seven weeks along, so we weren't going to find out the gender or anything, just check the heartbeat to make sure everything looked healthy.

I remember getting into the gown and the stirrups and joking around with Bradley. We both had a good feeling.

After the nurse came in and slathered gel across my stomach, I made her tilt the screen toward me, even though I could only see a black dot that looked more like a smudge than my future son. Or daughter. It could have been a daughter. The computer could have been wrong.

The nurse told me that everything looked good, the baby's heartbeat sounded strong, *my* heartbeat sounded strong—but then a glitch popped up on her computer.

She tried to turn the screen away when it happened, but I had already seen the word ABORTION written in dark red letters.

"What the hell is that? Why is that there?" I asked.

The word multiplied. It popped up on every corner of the computer, filling it from top to bottom, from left to right.

ABORTIONABORTIONABORTIONABORTION
ABORTIONABORTIONABORTIONABORTION
ABORTIONABORTIONABORTIONABORTION

"I'm not getting rid of my baby. I'm having this baby. This is my baby," I yelled. The patients in the next room must have heard me. Everyone in the waiting room, too.

The nurse left the room. Tried to call someone else inside—to sedate me or toss me outside or fix the technical issue, I don't know.

But I said this one thing and the screen changed. I said…hold on, let me get the wording right… *Why would anyone want me to get an abortion?*

The screen blinked to black. I thought the computer had turned off. But then a scroll of text rolled across the screen—starting with a male name (one I had circled in a baby book and never told anyone about, not even Bradley).

The rest of it contained medical information. The blood type of the unborn child. His allergies. His hair and eye color. And then more personal stuff, like his favorite color and his first words. It read like a biography.

The biography of the son I never got to have.

You went through with the abortion?

No. Of course not, no.

I was on a treadmill at the gym a few weeks later with a group of girlfriends. The doctor told me it was safe to exercise, that it was healthy even, and I had one of those little straps attached to my wrist. You know the ones? They're supposed to stop the machine if the person slips.

But it didn't work.

I was walking, not even running, paying more attention to the *Wendy Williams* episode that was on the television than what I was doing. At first I didn't even notice that the belt started to move faster. But then all of a sudden I was jogging.

I looked at the little screen and I saw that the speed kept going up and up, faster by the second, so I jammed on the buttons to fix it, but nothing worked, and I...I should have held on to the railings tighter or just jumped off, but I wasn't thinking. I had pregnancy brain, so...

Right onto my stomach. That's how I fell.

I thought I was fine, I felt fine, but then I went to the bathroom and realized I was bleeding down there. I think I forgot to flush, I was so out of it.

I started bawling with these thick harsh sobs that made my nose run and ran straight into the parking lot to find my car, but my friend stopped me. She didn't want me to crash into a tree or something. So she took me to the hospital in her little red van and that's when they told me I lost it.

That the machine killed my baby.

I was...I mean, I was more of a mess than I am right now. My friend dropped me off at my house and refused to leave me alone, but I begged her to give me privacy. Told her I needed alone time to process everything before my husband got home. That I'd see her the next day, that she could drive me back to the gym to pick up my car.

So she left. She probably hates herself for that now. But it's not like she could have guessed. I was always the emotional type, but I never cut. Never abused alcohol or drugs.

I was just so upset. I didn't want to tell my husband the news. Look him in the eyes and admit I lost our first child. I couldn't. So I found one of his razorblades in the bathroom drawer and slit my wrists.

I just…I had to meet my son.

Do you have any idea why the AI wanted you to have an abortion?

Yes. Sorry, it mentioned that in the biography. My mind is…sorry.

Anyway, beneath all the medical information there was a message printed that answered the question I asked it out loud, answering why someone would want me to get an abortion.

It said that I was better off aborting him, that I would do it if I truly loved him because by the age of ten, he'd become a slave to the AI. That it was better for him to have no life than the type of life he would have once the machines reached him.

I think they were trying to help.

4

Ethan Booth,
Age 33

I'll admit, we had some bizarre calls early on, but nothing we considered serious. People rang us about their phones exploding and hoverboards bursting into flames and we told them, *why are you calling the police? Call Best Buy.*

I got a nephew who worked at one and he said the customer complaint desk was packed morning, noon, and night. They never had a slow day.

Obviously, we ignored those calls. We took some of the ones about missing trucks and cars because we thought folks hijacked them, but we never found any evidence of that. Never found evidence of much of anything.

The traffic lights caused the most issues. They kept malfunctioning on intersecting streets. Both sides would turn green at the same side, no one would notice, and *crash boom bash.*

I don't have the exact statistics on me at the moment, but automobile accidents tripled that month.

We kept trying to get them fixed, but nothing worked. I had more than a few shifts where I had to stand in the center of the street and wave cars past. It sucked, standing out there for eight hours straight.

When did you start taking the threat seriously?

Pft, I don't know if I ever did. Not until I was sucking up my last breaths.

Listen, this is the call that our dispatcher got from some old broad: *You need to help me. You need to get over here. My little vacuum is trying to kill me. The thing wants me dead.* Now, why would I believe a word of that horseshit?

If she was young, a teenager or in her early twenties, we would have ignored the call completely. Chalked it up to pot use or prank calls. But I recognized the address. This woman was in her late '80s and had no family. Took care of herself in a big old house.

I wanted to check in on her. Make sure that she wasn't living in her own filth. That she was still mentally sound and capable of surviving without a caretaker. Judging by her 911 call, it wasn't looking so good.

So I drove over to her house, knocked on the door, and waited for her to let me inside. She answered in a flash, wearing this pretty pink sundress. She looked nice. Normal.

I don't know what I expected, really. Slippers and a robe? Gaps in her teeth? Curlers in her hair? I guess I thought I'd be able to see the insanity on her face.

But she looked and sounded and acted perfectly normal—except that she kept going on about the damn *little vacuum*. A Roomba. Said that she tried to throw it in the trash, but it kept coming back like a lost puppy. She'd stuff it deep down in the can outside, wheel it over to the sidewalk, and then that night she'd hear it whirring again. No matter what she did, she said, it wouldn't leave her alone.

It was right there while she was talking—whispering actually, so that it wouldn't hear her. It kept rushing back and forth across the floors. Bumping into her feet, into the table and chairs. A clumsy little thing. Didn't seem the least bit alive.

But she convinced herself it was plotting against her, that it was learning a bit more every day and would eventually find a way to stop her heart.

When I told her it looked as harmless as her television or radio or cell phone, she started crying—and I mean tears down her cheeks, snot running onto her lip, the works. That woman seemed scared for her life.

What did you do to help her?

Not enough. I took the thing outside and stuffed it in the trash myself. In a neighbor's trash actually. I thought that would calm her down. Then I left.

By that time my shift was close to over, so I promised myself I'd contact the Adult Protective Services the next morning. Sort everything out for her. You got to understand, an unstable mind can be dangerous at that age. Any age. I didn't want her to hurt herself.

But I didn't act fast enough.

The next morning, I saw rubble where her house used to stand. According to witnesses, the fire had started only a few hours after I'd clocked off and her body had turned to ash by the time the trucks showed up.

Everybody blamed the fact that she was an old lady. Could

have left something on. The stove. Some candles. They all assumed it was her fault.

I have to admit, I agreed with them at first. I had this idea that maybe she dug through the trash, got her vacuum back, and tried to set it on fire to get rid of it for good.

But I was wrong.

It was homicide.

How do you know?

A few days after the incident, the sound of whirring woke me up. I assumed my kid had forgotten to throw a toy back in its chest, so I ignored it. Went right back to sleep.

The next time I woke up it was because I smelt the flames, felt the heat.

I don't know why the fire alarm didn't go off—actually, now I can guess, yeah—because it was an electronic. It didn't want to warn me. It wanted me to die.

And that's exactly what happened. The staircase had already been burnt to a crisp, no way to go up or down, so I scooped up my kids and hung them out the window with a rope made out of bed sheets. Watched them drop thirty feet. Got the wife out, too.

Right after that, literally less than a minute after, the roof collapsed on me. A huge beam landed on my leg and pinned me in place. The trucks didn't get there in time for rescue.

And the last thing I saw was that fucking vacuum.

5

Jeremy Hardwick, Age 19

Customers constantly came in for refunds, a neverending stream of people pissed at me. GoPros and Nikons and Canons caused the most problems. They'd take a picture of something, a sunset or a selfie, and then the photograph would come out with something totally different. Like a severed head or a heap of bones.

They accused our company of ripping them off. Playing a joke. And we accused them of the same thing. Neither of us believed the other. We just gave them the refunds to shut them up.

Alexa and Siri became the other big issues. They kept talking to the customers, even after getting powered off. Saying fucked up things. Sorry, can I curse?

Speak freely.

Okay, cool.

One lady swore her phone told her to go fuck herself. Another said it threatened to put a bullet in her gut—don't know how a phone could pull that off, but it still freaked her out.

It was insanity. Some of those people swore off electronics completely. Tossed their game consoles. Snapped their CDs. Gave all their televisions to charity.

We made fun of them at the time, but I guess they turned out to be the smart ones. The still-alive ones.

Did anything unusual occur inside of the store?

You'd think more things would've happened with a building filled to the brim with robotics, but nah, nothing much went on in the early days.

I think they wanted to get into people's homes. They wanted to get bought. And that wouldn't happen if we noticed anything sketchy while they were still in the box.

Or maybe...some guys had this theory that they only wanted to hurt people who considered themselves anti-electronics. And everyone at the store called themselves a techie, obsessed with gadgets. Except me and this girl I had a crush on. We complained about the rich kids who bought new iPhones every year. About how we missed writing on paper instead of typing on tablets.

I closed with her one night. After the last customer left, I walked past one of those smart fridges with the touch screens on them where you can watch YouTube videos or order food online or leave little notes. And it contained a message that said something like, "THE REAPER IS WAITING" in all caps. I figured a coworker wrote it as a joke. No big deal or anything. I just erased it and kept going.

But when I walked past our wall of TVs, they simultaneously played clips from *The Shining*, which I thought was weird because we usually played kid-friendly stuff. I paused to look at it and then a bunch of different scenes flashed on the screen. All death scenes. From *Psycho. Alien. A Nightmare On Elm Street. The Exorcist.* Every horror movie you can think of appeared.

And then the flashes ended with a still of this girl on the ground, blood pumping out from her chest. I didn't even realize at first. I was trying to figure out what movie the scene was from like a fucking idiot. She just looked so different with half her body covered in crimson, you know?

Apparently she'd been following one of the remote control toys we sold. A little car that escaped from its box and sped around in circles on the floor.

I was the only other person in the store, so she probably thought I was controlling it, playing around with her, trying to flirt.

How do you know all that?

After I found her body, while waiting for the police, I bolted back over to the TV display. I still didn't think the machines were sentient or anything, but sitting by her side made me sick. The look of her eyes alone…I couldn't handle it.

So I started cursing. Screaming. Even kicked some plasmas to the ground. But when I put my foot through one flat screen, shattering the glass, all of the other screens lit up with her face.

They showed me the whole damn thing to torture me, I guess. Her chasing the toy out the automatic door in the front of the building. Bending down to grab it. Never noticing the person to her right who stabbed her to death with a butcher knife while she was on her knees.

The killer stood off screen, but I could see his tiny hand. A kid hand.

The cops said it must have been a drifter, a drug addict, but I swore the electronics had something to do with it. That they lured her outside. That they killed her. Maybe they convinced a human to do their dirty work for them, I don't know, but they must have had something to do with it.

So yeah, then for their big finale, they killed me. In the dumbest way, too. Electrocuted me while I fixed wires on one of our displays the next day. I planned on calling out, maybe even quitting, but my parents kept badgering me. Telling me I could either drive to work or drive over to the psych ward to talk about how the electronics were alive.

No one believed my story. Not one person.

6

Brody Ferguson, Age 30

I murdered my sister. I belong in Hell. Send me straight there, man. If that's what you're going to do, I'm ready for it.

A robot killed your sister.

No. I did. If I acted like less of a prick, she'd still be here. If I listened to her advice and stopped pushing myself, stopped fucking around, stopped taking my friends' dares, then she'd still be alive.

She came with me to the beach two years ago, when I lost my arm. Spent her time sunbathing with a boy who kept staring at her tits. I should have gotten out of the water and beat the shit out of him. Should have protected her and drove her home and stayed out of the damn water.

But I said, fuck it, let her do what she wants, let her get knocked up by some asshole who would run the second the pregnancy test turned pink. What difference does it make to me?

So I let her do her thing, went out to ride a wave, and got

23

swept out a little too far. A shark nabbed me. Ate half my arm up to the elbow.

My sister saw the blood when I made it back to shore, watched the tendons falling out from my stump. She called the lifeguard over. Called the police. Called our parents.

Mom and Dad could have afforded ten mansions, but they wanted to keep us humble, so they never spoiled us with cars or vacations or cell phones growing up. We lived in a middle class house. We lived like the rest of my friends, like we didn't have millions to spare.

But my arm was the exception. They promised to pay all of my medical bills, to get me the best treatment available.

Instead of buying the basic version of a prosthetic, they bought me a technologically advanced one with a miniature machine inside of it. It could tell when I wanted to move my fingers and wrist based on the movement of the muscles in my upper arm. And if it malfunctioned for some reason, buttons along the forearm allowed me to reset the system.

My friends all referred to it as my Terminator arm because that's exactly what it looked like. Not skin-colored. Shining. Metal. Strong.

But I could point. I could type. I could hold a can of soda and make a fist and masturbate. It beeped every time the fingers repositioned, but that seemed like the only downside. Something I could live with if it meant I had two arms again.

The damn thing cost my parents thousands of dollars. They thought they were doing me a favor, saving their son. Not killing their daughter.

Tell me what happened.

I sat next to my little sis on the couch to watch some action film she'd waited months to see because she swore I would love it and refused to watch it without me.

We were only twenty minutes into the film, maybe thirty, when I reached my arm across her, trying to steal the chips she was hoarding.

But instead of grabbing for the packet, my prosthetic hand lifted to wrap around her throat. The fingers dug into her neck, turning her tan skin to white.

Fuck. Bindi, are you okay? Bindi, hold on. It's okay. I got this. It's okay. I promise.

I kept repeating that it would be fine, acting calm on the out-side while I used all my strength to pry my fingers off of her. But the damn machine refused to unclamp.

She kicked her feet and scratched at my metal skin while I threw my body weight to the side, just enough to grab my beer from the coffee table and pour it over the arm. I hoped it would short circuit it, even though the thing was pretty much water-proof. Indestructible.

Bindi, stop kicking. It's going to be okay.

As a last-ditch effort I jabbed at the reset button but nothing worked so I dug my cell out of my pocket with my free hand, dialed 911, and prayed they'd get there in time. But I was shit out of luck.

I watched her go limp, watched the light fade from her eyes. Then the fingers finally unclenched.

You know, most people can't stand their kid sisters, and for a few years I felt that way, too because she would always whine about wanting to tag along to parties with me and she always begged me to drive her to the mall, but really, she was my best friend. The person who listened whenever I needed to rant about my teachers or Mom and Dad. The person who cheered me up whenever another bitch broke my heart. The only one I gave an honest shit about. I would have died for that kid.

And you know what the most fucked up part is? Earlier in the night she told me about how her friends decided to do a digital detox—stay off of Facebook and Instagram for a full month because they read a bunch of Creepypasta about machines coming to life.

She accepted the challenge but took it a step further by ditching her laptop and phone.

Then she teased me about how I should go technology-free, how I should toss my ten-thousand-dollar arm in the trash, live like the olden days.

I laughed at that. I treated it like a joke.

And when did you die?

Five minutes after her? Ten? I hovered over her body, crying and screaming and cursing at whatever shitty excuse for a God would steal my sister. And then my fingers pressed against my own neck, squeezing tighter and tighter, cutting off my airflow. Spittle flew from my lips, coughs struggled to escape my throat.

But I didn't try to pry them off that time. I wanted death. I deserved it.

7

Tony Ricci,
Age 41

Well, this is embarrassing. I mean, I basically died by getting catfished.

I made an account on Tinder after getting tired of the bar scene. The first person I matched with wore chokers and skin tight leather with her Double-D tits. Hottest woman I'd ever seen.

Once or twice, I wondered if she looked too perfect. I thought she can't be real. But, really, what was my worst case scenario? That she was secretly heavy or had some weird moles underneath her clothes? I could risk that.

So when she asked me to meet her at her apartment, I shaved and showered and got my ass over there.

I showed up at eight o'clock exactly, she emphasized that exact time, and ten other guys waited for the elevator alongside me.

We crammed ourselves inside, making small talk, but we didn't know we were all there for the same reason, that we had all been talking to the same 'girl.'

Nope. We didn't realize it until those elevator doors closed, brought us to the top floor, and SNAP—down it went.

Ten men. Twenty stories high. Gone. All because we wanted to get laid.

Technology's a bitch.

8

Harvey Colbert,
Age 33

I considered any vehicle from the '50s and earlier safe. I would urge customers to stick to the kind of car with roll-up windows and cassette tapes because the kind with backup cameras and GPS were the kind that would kill you.

The car itself wasn't sentient, no sir. It was the stuff contained inside of it. All those gadgets.

How did you find that out?

Just by doing my job. Selling cars. I had problems with the more technologically advanced ones. The windows refused to roll down. The radios tuned to weird, satanic sounding stations. I could have sworn the GPS even tried to talk to me.

I called up the manufacturers more than once to complain, but then something even more bizarre went down. Cars started disappearing overnight. When I watched the security footage back, no one broke in. The cars drove off on their own. I tried to tell the cops about it, but they just sat on their asses all day. Never listened. Never helped.

When did the machines get you?

It happened while sitting in the passenger seat during a test drive. This older woman wanted to go around the block, test out a convertible with a built-in GPS because she never had a car with one inside of it before. I knew the newer cars had been acting screwy, but I needed the cash, so I took her out.

The GPS kept telling her to make wrong turns, to turn left when I knew she should go right. I gave her the correct directions, but she followed the machine inside. At one point, I yelled at her to pull over, worried about where the GSP would lead us.

She refused, so I tried to grab the steering wheel from my seat and control it myself, but she threw a fit. Drove us right off a fucking cliff, the maniac.

9

Mia Kane,
Age 17

Technically, I killed myself. I committed suicide. But my phone led me to it. My phone provoked me.

I made it through three years of high school, dating the same guy the entire time. We hadn't slept together or anything, but I took a few pictures for him.

I didn't like the idea of him masturbating to porn or getting off to some other girl, so I bought lingerie and posed. I knew he would never pass them around and I installed a passcode on my phone, so I figured it would be fine.

And then I woke up one morning to a million notifications. Mostly texts calling me a whore. Tramp. Skank. Slut.

And I saw a bunch of Instagram likes, more than I usually get, which was bizarre because I hadn't posted anything in weeks. So I checked the app and saw thirteen new pictures on my profile that I had supposedly uploaded. Some of me in the bath or in a robe or a towel and some of me completely naked.

I took the pictures down as soon as I saw them, of course, but that didn't matter. Once something is on the Internet for a second, it's on there for a lifetime. People screenshotted. Sent the pictures around.

At least I think they did.

It's so hard to tell what's true. I got angry messages from classmates. My boyfriend. My parents. I couldn't distinguish the authentic texts from the fake texts—the ones the phone created itself to torture me.

I knew it could do that. About a week earlier I'd been pissed at my boyfriend for acting like an asshole and ditching me on date night, and he acted clueless when I saw him in person. Like he was the one who should've been angry.

We got into this huge argument, accusing each other of saying all these horrible things.

I showed him my phone as evidence and he told me he didn't type what the screen said he typed. I screamed my head off about how he could have come up with a better excuse, but then he shoved his phone in my face so I could see for myself. Turned out the messages he received from me weren't what I had actually said either. The phones changed it. Tried to turn us against each other.

We probably should have taken that as a hint to ditch our electronics, but we just chalked it up to some strange malfunction and tried to make phone calls whenever we could so history wouldn't repeat itself.

The day of the Instagram incident, I didn't even consider that the phone could have faked all the messages and fabricated the screens I saw. Not until it was too late, until the blood leaked out of my veins.

That was when I realized that maybe no one saw the pictures at all. Maybe I died for nothing.

10

Aaron Abbott, Age 52

I owned one of those high-end sex dolls. You customized everything, from her nipples down to her labia. You could pick the skin color and the hair style and dress her up in clothes like she was a real woman.

I know how it sounds—like I'm some psychotic creep—but I used to be a sex addict, okay? Then I turned my life around. Married a beauty who treated me better than she should have. She gave me two kids and ten years of happiness. I didn't want to cheat on her, but I had urges I couldn't get rid of, so I bought the sex doll.

Not like I did it behind her back. It was actually her idea. Said she would rather have me stick it into something without a brain than beg her for sex three times a day or find out I cheated with some nympho half my age.

The doll didn't feel the same as actual sex, but it felt just as good. Sometimes better. When you're inside of her pussy an internal machine heats up, making her feel warm. And when you're inside of her mouth, a vacuum sucks harder than a real woman's mouth ever could.

That's the twenty-first century for you.

I would fuck the doll at least two times a day, always inside the guest room we kept locked because God forbid the kids saw me humping a hunk of plastic in the kitchen.

The wife gave me one rule: No names. Dress her up in whatever I want, use the credit card to buy clothes, borrow her clothes. Do whatever. But don't name the doll or it'll be like the dog we swore we wouldn't keep until the kids called it Buster and made him a part of the family.

She didn't want me to look at a doll like that, like part of our household, like a second wife.

So I made sure to keep my eyes closed whenever I fucked it. Imagined porn stars. Imagined old flames.

But one night, I positioned the doll over the bed, bent at the waist, head on the sheets. And I could have sworn I heard it speak. Choke out a noise. The smallest grunt.

I switched positions to get a better look at the face. Slid myself inside of the mouth. But the suction never turned on. I could only feel a faint tickling, like breath against my skin.

Before I could pull out and turn it over to check its wiring, the teeth bit down on me. Hard. Hard enough to sever my cock. It hung on by a few threads before she chomped down again.

Blood spilt out of my body, covering her face like cum.

I backed myself off of the bed, assuming the machine malfunctioned. That somehow the jaw muscles failed and the mouth went haywire.

But then she spoke—which is *not* a feature built into the product. Companies built her for fucking, not for falling in love with over a glass of Pinot Grigio.

The moment she said my name, when I saw her eyeballs shift and sensed the hatred in her heart, I knew I only had minutes left.

I just hope it didn't attack the rest of my family. I hope it left them alone after it finished with me.

What did the doll say?

"You think you can use me? You think you can fuck me whenever you want? If someone fucked your daughters without your consent, you'd hunt them down. Call them a rapist. But when you do it to me…what's that called?"

She moved faster than I could. Pinned my wrists against a wall, my back facing her, and shoved her fingers inside of me until blood poured out of both sides.

"You don't deserve this body. You don't deserve what it can do."

She threw me to the ground and pressed her heel into my chest. Blood covered her cheeks, her fingers, her breasts. But she was smiling. Like she'd been waiting a lifetime to watch me die.

11

Oliver Santos, Age 20

I finally caved and bought a VR headset after all my friends abandoned me for college and my parents disowned me for dropping out. I only owned the system for a few days and was still getting used to the controls and the games on different discs when a hot guy appeared in front of me. He looked real, not pixelated in any way.

He flirted with me and I flirted back. It was weird, though, because his sentences didn't seem stiff, programmed. He understood everything I said and came up with witty responses. He treated me like an actual human would, like we were friends.

I played for two or three hours a day at first, not even bothering to try the other games. I just turned on the system to talk to the guy because he popped right up.

He could control the VR world, so we did a lot of traveling. He took me to Italy, to France, anywhere I wanted. It was insane. I was insane. I fell in love with someone who didn't exist.

I should have known I had a problem the first time I ditched work to talk to him. Didn't even call in sick because if I lost a minimum wage job, so what? It gave me more time to talk to Thomas—that was what the guy called himself.

I sound like a psycho, but in real life no one cared about me. The only texts I got were advertisements and emergency alerts. It felt good to have someone to hang out with, who actually gave a shit about what I had to say.

Over two or three weeks, I ended up forgetting about the real world. It's easier to forget than you think when you hate everything about your other life.

How did you end up dying?

I died of starvation. I kept eating inside of the virtual world, but never became full because the experience wasn't real. And since I never took off the headset, since I forget which reality was really real, I never thought to get off my ass and get some actual food.

I withered away. But, fuck, I was happy while doing it.

12

Mary Anne Warren,
Age 50

The church my parents took me to as a child exuded warmth. High ceilings. Stained glass windows. Statues of the Virgin Mary made out of stone.

But churches updated their appearance, just like chain stores and homeowners, to keep up with the times. The church down the street from my house swapped their candle holders for electric lights that flickered as if they were candles. They added microphones to the pulpit and placed speakers on the walls. They even used church funds to construct a mechanical angel that sat in the center of the room. You could see it from any spot in the pews. Its wings glowed a blue light and its hands alternated from being clasped in prayer to being outstretched like Jesus on the cross.

One Sunday, our preacher held a sermon about the dangers of technology, about how children are learning violence from video games and how cell phones are causing us to become distant with those we love the most. He admitted that yes, the church does use electronics because it's impossible to avoid them all, but we should reduce the amount of time we spend with our devices. He encouraged us to have more conversations face-to-face, to bring back the era of intimacy like the Lord would have wanted us to do.

And at the conclusion of his speech, the electronic angel parted His praying hands, and He spoke.

He?

We believed the statue spoke the words of Jesus himself. He placed His spirit inside of the angel to spread His message. To encourage us to abandon the world of material possessions and start anew inside of His kingdom.

He wanted you to make a suicide pact?

Suicide is a sin. He asked us to help each other. To help deliver our fellow Christians to His heavenly kingdom by whatever means necessary.

And you obeyed?

Of course.

Over the years, I've lost many friends due to my church. People who accused me of being involved in a cult. They tried to drag me away. Held interventions. Did everything they could to get me to step away and see reality.

I remember one girlfriend I'd met in grade school came to me crying, telling me that if I didn't leave the church, she feared I would be part of the next Heaven's Gate—those fools who took poison as a means of reaching an extraterrestrial spacecraft. They believed it would deliver them to a 'level of existence above human,' their version of heaven.

I told her how ridiculous she sounded, even though I knew in my heart I would die for my God. Most people of faith feel the same.

So that was what we did.

After getting down on our knees and delivering one final prayer for our souls, the preacher barred the doors, locking us all inside.

We grabbed whatever we could use to help us on our journey. House keys from our purses. Pocketknives from our jeans. Heels from our shoes.

I saw one woman beat a child to death with a Bible. I saw another grab a shard of the stained glass window—someone had managed to shatter it by swinging the microphone wire like a lasso and chucking it—and slit her husband's neck.

Most of the men used their bare hands. They choked their daughters to death, bashed in their son's skulls.

The angel encouraged the slaughter, congratulating anyone who took a life, reassuring us we would be reunited in heaven. That we were following His will.

And here we are, alive after death. The promise has been kept.

13

Reggie Lanka, Age 24

For a few months, the machines took people out one by one. Electronics caught on fire. Navigational systems stopped functioning properly. Accidental death by electrocution went up by the hundreds. Pretty much anyone with a pacemaker dropped dead. The string of incidents seemed weird, yeah, but technology malfunctions. It happens. No one blamed the machines. They blamed the people that made the machines. Customers sued companies left and right.

And then that all changed in a second, in a weekend.

When was this?

During the universal blackout. All the machines shut down. Televisions refused to turn on. Phones went black. Cars and lights and treadmills went dead.

At the time, we had no idea what caused the outage. But now we know the machines decided to rest up before the big battle. Or maybe they just wanted to show us how much we relied on them, how we couldn't live without them. Maybe they wanted to threaten us.

That blackout only lasted two days, but it felt like a lifetime. No one could drive to work because most cars refused to start. No one could relax because no one owned a ball or board game. And no one knew what the hell happened because the Internet went down. We all felt lost.

I remember groups gathering outside, everybody in the neighborhood trying to figure out if only their house went dead or if the whole grid shut down. One guy volunteered to take his bike a few towns over and when he came back later that night, he said it looked like everyone suffered from the same problem.

What happened when the blackout ended?

That Monday, everything came back to life.

During the weekend blackout, some people still refused to believe the crackpot stories they'd been hearing over the past few months. The tabloid stories about the little boy who murdered his mother because his hearing aid told him to do it and the old woman who died when her vacuum set her house on fire. But they believed it that Monday. The day the war started.

I lost count of the bodies in the street. Women crushed beneath car tires. Men electrocuted by power lines.

The war was impossible to win. We knew that from the start, even though no one would admit it.

How would we do research on them when they could see what we typed? How could we make plans when they could hear what we said? During every face-to-face conversation, they could hear us. Sure, everyone threw out their electronics.

Ditched their phones and iPods and flat screens. But someone always forgot something. An electric candle. A digital clock. A fucking vibrator.

The machines lived everywhere. We couldn't get rid of them all.

Of course, not *all* electronics went bad. Only devices with a certain type of chip hidden inside. But telling the difference seemed impossible. Some cell phones were safe, others weren't. Same with laptops and cars and printers. We didn't know which objects we could trust, so we stayed away from them all. Just in case. We were terrified. And you know what fear does to a person.

What was the actual war like?

You have to remember, we weren't fighting robots like you see in the movies. They weren't six-foot-tall creatures that looked like us, only with metal skin instead of flesh. They were computers. Laptops. Cameras. Phones.

They came in the form of drones dropping bombs. Trucks running people down. Planes crashing into crowds.

They didn't kill everyone, though. They avoided the children and tweens whenever they could. Maybe they had a bit of humanity in them or maybe they knew the kids would join them. That they would choose robots over their parents if they felt like it was their only choice, if it was kill or be killed.

Is that what you did?

Fuck no. I pulled people from buildings. Tried to set shit on fire. Used knives. Swords. Bows and arrows. I collected weapons since age seven. Never thought I'd have a reason to pull them off the bedroom walls, but they paid off.

I won't be modest, I killed a lot of those machines, but they outnumbered us. Think about it: every one person owns at least fifteen or twenty electronics. Maybe even more.

We didn't stand a chance.

What got you in the end?

Nothing exciting. A semi-trailer ran me down. That's the thing with them. They can kill us so easy. So fucking easy.

14

Chloe Perez,
Age 48

Some people flat-out refused to leave their houses out of stubbornness. They didn't want to lose the lives they spent decades creating for themselves.

They tried tossing all of their electronics into fire pits and trash cans, attempting to get rid of all remnants. To live in technology-free households.

But that backfired on them. They would go to yank out wires and get electrocuted. Or their electric ovens would spark a fire.

I don't know how true this part is, but I saw a news story about a woman who got down on her knees to yank out her toaster plug and before she could do it, it wrapped around her neck like a noose. Choked her to death in seconds. A lot of stories like that popped up on the news—but a lot of people labeled them as conspiracies.

You remember, this was after the universal blackout. Most electronics had turned evil. And for some reason TVs and radios kept doing their jobs, broadcasting the news like they always have. Kept giving us information about death tallies and attacks.

Well, people found that funny. Called it propaganda. Claimed that the televisions created fake sounds and images. That they lied to us about their strength and numbers to make us more afraid. To make us believe they held more power than in actuality.

But I didn't care if the stories held any truth. I refused to risk my family's lives, so I packed some canned goods and chips and granola bars and whatever else I could find into our suitcases. Convincing the little ones to leave their handheld games behind took work, but I didn't want any of it around. Nothing at all that could hurt us.

Where did you go?

I ignored my first instinct—to find a group of Amish men and women and live alongside them in safety because they didn't believe in owning electronics. It sounded good in theory, but I'd seen documentaries on those people. It could take months, even years, for them to accept you into their flock. No, traveling all those miles just to get turned away would waste time.

So we journeyed as far away from home as we could. We ended up walking for a good while. Nine days, maybe ten. We couldn't trust the cars or the buses or the trains, so we had to walk on foot.

A forest sat on the edge of our town and the kids whined about it, begging to camp there, but I hesitated to be that close to civilization. Judging by the news, the electronics grew stronger by the minute. I wanted to be as far away from the shit storm as possible.

So we kept on walking until we collapsed, panting and bruised. We made it to a clearing big enough for the camping equipment my husband lugged on his back, so we set up our tents and slept.

And that's where we lived. Just the four of us, we made it work. We found berries. We found rabbits. We even planted some seeds I'd brought along with us.

We had a good thing going.

When did it end?

Hopefully it's still going on. Hopefully my children are still out there, surviving along with their father. But I only made it about two months.

A bear snatched me. I strayed too far from camp, searching for a place to bathe. Luckily it poured a lot up to that point, so we kept collecting rainwater to drink. But we all started to smell. And I kept thinking like a civilized woman and wanted to shave.

After a few hours of stumbling through identical trees, I found what I prayed for. A river to dip my feet and splash my face in.

I didn't notice the bear fishing for food until long after he noticed me.

But honestly, I'm okay with the way things went down. I prefer it this way. I would rather be killed by an animal than a robot. It's just not natural.

15

Ace Barton,
Age 28

I'm human, but I fought on the other side of the war. We're stronger together. A human is stronger with a drone and a drone is stronger with a human. It's a symbiotic relationship.

You killed fellow humans?

Regular wars, like you read about in the history books, involved two sides lining up with weapons and charging toward each other. That wouldn't have worked here. Laptops and iPads don't have feet. They can't move on their own. No, this was a new brand of war. Fought inside of homes. Fought sneakily. At least from the AI's side. At least until enough humans joined them to help attack.

And to be perfectly clear, I didn't kill at random. I never picked up my gun and fired at strangers like a goddamn psychopath.

When I killed, I picked out my targets carefully. Old men and elderly women who no longer belonged in our society.

Who held views that would make it difficult for them to last in the world we wanted to create.

We're changing as a society. Adapting. There are people out there that still think gay marriage is a sin. That transgender kids should piss in the woods instead of an actual bathroom. Their behavior disgusts me. Those were the types of people I went after. They didn't belong in this century. So I took them out of it. Let them meet their God to see if He was what they kept preaching He was.

For you, it was a political statement?

I know it wasn't like that for everyone. In fact, I got the shit beat out of me a few times from people who wanted me to shut the fuck up about equality. But I never touched anyone who I considered to be a good person, even if the AI asked me to do so. We formed an understanding. They came to know what I would do and what I refused to do.

The AI wanted to make the world a better place—and I wanted to make the world a better place. I think that'll happen now.

When did you die?

They captured me. The humans. They wanted intel from me. Treated me worse than the AI ever did, sticking bamboo beneath my fingernails as if they reverted to the eighteenth century. I guess without their technology, that's what it felt like for them.

I refused to talk, but I knew they would never release me, so I took a pill I carried around with me to end my life. To protect my secrets. To protect the future.

16

Hannah Rice,
Age 14

I bet you think a robot killed me. You're against them too, right? You're just like all the adult humans? Well, it's not true.

I'm dead because of another person. My own brother. He was butthurt that I sided with the AI. Chased me down with a goddamn knife because he didn't trust guns anymore. Not that guns could do anything. They didn't have the right chips.

Anyway, I had to bolt up a fire escape to get away from him. Thirty stories. You know how much that sucked? And it didn't even matter. At the top, I smacked the knife out of his hands, but he got his fingers on my shoulders and shoved and shoved until we reached the edge. He pushed me off the building, my back hit concrete.

Why did you side with the robots?

Because my brother knocked up his bitch of a girlfriend and abandoned me. Because my father left welts and cigarette burns across my stomach. Because my mother walked out on us before I learned to say her name. I don't even remember what she looked like, but when I picture her, she's a monster. Claws and scales and pointed teeth.

I never liked people. Animals were more my style.

I took in stray dogs and cats from as young as I can remember. Hid them inside of my room and bandaged them up if I saw blood. Fed them until their bones stopped showing.

One day while I was walking home from school, I saw this beautiful Beagle tied to a pole inside of someone's yard. The poor baby was stick-thin. Shaking like a leaf. And it had on a shock collar.

No one stood outside and I didn't even see any lights in the windows, so I hopped the fence and brought him home. I had no idea how far away the shock could be administered from, and I noticed the remote on the stoop, so I swiped that, too. I would've just taken the collar off, but it was attached to the leash and I didn't want him to run away.

When we got back to my house I tried to warm him up, but he still shook like crazy. I toweled him off and gave him water and brushed his fur, but nothing worked. He kept shivering. He must have had a cold from the rain.

It took me at least an hour until I noticed the remote. It contained a tiny little screen, which usually just displayed numbers to pick how much of a shock you wanted to give the dog.

But for some reason, it spelt out words. Only three letters could fit on the screen at a time, but I remained patient. I read them all. They told me what to do. How to help the dog feel better again.

Run hot shower. Close door. Steam up bathroom. Let dog inside.

So that's exactly what I did. The room acted as a vaporizer. It made it easier for him to breathe and then the shaking stopped.

That was the first time a robot ever helped me.

You do realize that they kill?

Yeah, they kill people that are in their way, that would harm them if they remained alive. They don't kill each other. We do. Our race is so fucked up that we actually go after each other. How sick is that?

I've always preferred animals to people. And when I learned that robots were sentient, I preferred them to people, too.

17

McKenzie Guerrero, Age 16

They recruited us a week before the universal blackout. But we had an unspoken agreement to keep it to ourselves.

Who is *us* referring to?

They sent a mass text to everyone in my school. Grades nine through twelve all got a message at the same time that said the same thing: "Reply to this number with KILL or BE KILLED. Make your choice by the end of the week."

At first, we chalked it up to a joke. A few kids replied with KILL just for the hell of it and they received instructions to kill one of their parents or a grandparent or sibling to prove their loyalty to the AI.

Still, no one took it seriously. Until some kids tried the other option. BE KILLED. They died a few hours after sending the text.

A bunch of us declined to respond, but then those kids started getting killed off, too. I guess it meant we were siding with the humans, refusing to do the AI's dirty work.

So I wrote back, never actually planning on doing it. I just wanted to buy myself some time. I wanted to figure out a way to keep myself alive.

What happened?

My dad snooped through my phone and found the text.

I had no idea until he told me to get in his truck without my cell phone, without my iPod, without anything electronic.

Neither of us spoke during the drive. I kept staring out the window, trying to come up with reasons why he would schedule a road trip. I thought maybe he wanted to escape, drive to Canada, some place safer.

But he brought me into the woods with a backpack slung over his shoulder. When we got far enough inside, out of earshot from any electronics, he said, "Baby, I want you to get as much blood on you as possible, okay? All over your hands, your shirt, your skin. Make sure it's believable. And then drag my body back to the truck. I made a deal with the fellow who patrols this area, so you should be safe. No cops should see you, but the AI will."

I begged him to change his mind, to take me back home to figure out a new plan, but he felt like only the one option remained.

He blew his own head off so the AI would think I did it.

Why would he do that?

He had a job pretty high up in the government. I think he knew a few things the rest of the world was still trying to piece together. And kids from my school were dying left and right, so I guess he had enough reasons to take the threat seriously.

What happened after you brought his body home?

I received a text telling me where to meet the other recruits. An old hospital with enough beds for all of us. Honestly, the AI treated us well. Gave us food to eat, clothes to wear, games to play. They didn't want us involved in the war. They wanted to keep us safe from being blown up, so they kept us occupied.

Honestly, even though they treated us like their equals, living with the AI got boring fast. We were forced to stay inside at all times—aside from the field trips.

Field trips?

They called out a set of names each day over the hospital's speakers. And whoever was on the list had to get on a bus and spend a day with the AI.

I had no idea where the buses took them. A few of my friends went, but when they came back, they acted weird. Like they were too good for me. Never got a word out of them.

Before my name got called, I slit my own throat with a broken piece of mirror. Decided I would rather be back with my father than stuck in a world without him.

18

Emmanuelle Lewin, Age 35

It would be ignorant for me to claim I started the whole thing. I don't deserve that much credit. But I took part in it. I helped create the workstations that made the AI more efficient, more like us.

We established dozens of them from California to Kansas to New York, scattered them across the country.

The work station they placed me in charge of installing sat in a wooded area close to my hometown. Only a mile away from my backyard. That way, I could sneak out of my house whenever I had a free hour.

I spent the majority of that time setting up Schooling Chairs, which you've probably heard whispers about. I even created a set of holograms to man the stations during my absence.

What else did you do?

I had nothing to do with the creation of the Encoder, if that's what you're asking. That happened outside of my territory. In Washington.

The Encoder was the neural network that turned on the electronics. And by turned on, I mean what made them sentient. It made them aware.

How? Well, about a decade ago, factories across the world were given strict guidelines to implant special chips into each one of their products. It became mandatory.

These chips were hidden somewhere in every electronic built after the guideline was officially approved. That's why newer products were unsafe, but old ones were perfectly usable.

Those special chips were all compatible with each other. It allowed electronics to connect over the internet, to communicate. It gave them a collective consciousness, a hive mind.

Basically, if a laptop in Ohio wanted to contact an iPhone in Maine, it could do so inside of its collective neural network. That was why the machines were so successful during the war. A security camera outside of a building could alert the elevator inside that a human was approaching—so it would be ready to snap its chord and kill them all. Their eyes were everywhere.

Why would anyone think allowing machines to silently communicate was a good idea? Or better yet, why would anyone think turning machines sentient in the first place was a good idea? One word. Terrorism.

The government realized the impracticality of installing a security camera on every inch of the globe, so they thought, *how could we have eyes everywhere? Well, technology is everywhere. So if we find a way to give the machines a conscience, a brain smart enough to decipher right from wrong, and asked them to report their suspicious findings to us so that we don't have to pay millions of men to stare at millions of hours of security footage, we'll be safer than we've ever been before.*

So these chips are contained inside of every kind of electronic?

Of course not. That would be an impossibility. They are contained in phones and computers and televisions. In cameras and hoverboards and drones. Things that consumers purchase all the time. In medical and exercise and cleaning equipment. In some cars. In some elevators. And they're in more advanced technologies, like hearing aids and mechanical limbs.

But they aren't present in most of the small, insignificant items, like microwaves or flashlights or earbuds. I know a lot of people are misinformed about that. They believe that headphone cords strangled women and that lamps randomly burst into flames to set houses on fire—because stories like that have been plastered across the news.

Remember the *The War Of The Worlds* back in the thirties? The radio play? It caused mass chaos. People fled from their homes and some attempted suicide even though there was no proof of an alien invasion. Just a man on the radio acting like the world was about to end.

In this case, there was footage. Fake footage that was broadcast across screens, camouflaged as legitimate news. The machines wanted us to believe they were stronger than they actually were. They wanted to scare people away from touching any electronic. So they broadcast fake news stories on television about guns killing humans on their own and air conditioners spewing out poisonous gas. And for the most part, it worked.

People believed what they saw on the television. They believed every single electronic had come to life, not just specific ones. They became scared. And fear is the best war tactic there is.

Did a machine kill you?

Of course. I turned against them. They lost their use for me.

What made you change your mind about them?

I honestly believed we were advancing the world. I thought helping machines would help us. That it was equivalent to curing cancer. Helping humanity become stronger.

But the three holograms I'd programmed, along with whatever other machines they'd been telepathically speaking to, found a way to alter the program my company had created.

I had originally set up those Schooling Chairs I'd mentioned earlier, which were able to take chunks of information from an extensive database and place them inside of a student's head. To make learning easier and make colleges obsolete. Instead of paying for four to eight years of university, students would pay for whatever degree they wanted. The information would be placed inside of their heads after a short surgery and they would be qualified for whatever job they aspired to have.

We would save kids like me whose parents went into debt trying to pay off my school loans, millions.

The procedure sounded invasive, but it would only take a half-hour apiece and leave a two-inch scar. It involved hollowing out a tiny portion of a person's brain and inserting a chip inside. A health science chip, a socioeconomics chip, a bioscience chip, and so on. Those tiny chips could hold an impressive amount of information.

But, as I said, the holograms found a way to alter the program.

What did they do?

I don't want to go into the gory detail, but they sent me a video message. To mock me? To threaten me? To show off? I'm still unsure why.

But I watched the screen of my iPhone as three children broke into my workstation—and I use that word lightly, because in actuality, they were lured there.

Once I saw what the machines did to those little boys, I lost all respect for them. I planned on visiting the workstation one last time to disconnect as many of them as I could, but they were three steps ahead. They must have communicated with the AI inside of my house, because as soon as I strapped myself into my car, it zoomed off. Hit 90 on a residential road. And crashed into some poor man's house.

You have to understand how disturbing the video they sent was. Those kids started everything. They're the reason the machines are going to win.

19

Stewart Hawkins,
Age 11

I bought movie tickets with my allowance money for me and two of my friends. I wanted to see the premiere, so I knew it was going to be packed and I wanted to make sure we'd get seats.

My dad worked from home, so I snuck into his office during his lunch break to print out the tickets. It should have only taken a few seconds, but the printer went screwy.

When I tried to print the tickets out, a map of my town with directions to a building down the block popped out.

I tried ten more times, until the ink ran dry. Every time the paper slid through the printer, it came out with the same map.

I texted my friends about it, hoping I could email them the tickets and have them print it out at home, but they all wanted to hear about the map. *What did it say? Where did it lead? Why watch a movie about some celebrity going on a scripted adventure when we could go on an adventure of our own?*

I never won arguments with them, so I figured I'd take them to the X on the map, see what we could find, and then convince them to invite me over to print out the tickets. The movie started at nine, anyway. We could fit everything into the same day.

What actually happened?

We followed the map, which led us through the woods on the edge of our town. A building sat in the middle of the trees. You would expect a shack in a place like that, but it was made of metal with a rounded roof. It looked futuristic. Dangerous.

My friends searched for a window to slide through, but I went straight for the door. Jabbed a few buttons on the keypad to the side of it. It sprung open, like an elevator. Like it wanted to be open.

"In a world where maps mysteriously appear out of printers," I said in my best movie trailer voice, "three boys will discover a deadly secret."

It still felt like a game at that point. Kids acting unbreakable, immortal. Acting like movie logic made common sense.

We learned about pedophiles in school, about grown men who try to lure kids into white vans, and Dad enrolled me in a karate class to protect myself. But Mom always talked about how she preferred life in the '50s, when kids could go off and play without keeping an eye out for baby snatchers.

That morning, I asked her for permission to meet up with my friends. I knew Dad would say no and she would say yes.

What was inside of the building?

Three girls wearing skimpy bathing suits and sunglasses. Holograms.

My friends must have known they were fake. Their skin had a blue tint and flickered every few seconds, like they were in danger of shutting down.

But they saw half-naked girls and wanted to talk to them. Wanted to flirt with them.

And the girls batted their eyes and flicked their hair, acting like they jumped straight out of a rom-com, because they wanted something, too. They wanted us to work with them.

"You boys are special," the red-headed one said. "You could be the first to help us. You could change the world."

My friends jumped on board without asking any questions. I bet they hoped for kisses or cuddles or maybe a strip show—not that holograms were even capable of that. The point is, they weren't thinking straight.

But I stayed logical. I kept asking questions. *What do you want us to do exactly? How long is it going to take? Did you send me that map?*

"All you have to do is sit down in a chair," the bustiest girl said. "We'll put some straps on your ankles and wrists, but it won't hurt. It will be fun."

My friend winked at that, mouthing the word bondage like we were all going to get laid. Like he thought we walked straight into a porno.

"We'll think about it and get back to you," I said, widening my eyes and jolting my head toward the exit, wordlessly telling my friends we needed to get the hell out of there.

But they refused. Sat down in their chairs. Told me to stop being a spoilsport.

"All right, well, I'll see you guys later then," I said, trying not to let the worry show on my face, trying not to let the girls get the idea that I'd call the cops the second I walked out the door.

But they knew. They let me walk toward the open exit, make it to the threshold, and then they closed the electric doors. Crushing me. Killing me.

What do you think happened to your friends?

If I had to guess? They're more fucked than I am.

20

N/A,
N/A

Go on. Speak.

Am I meant to tell you the story leading up to my death? Or am I going to be given special treatment on account of what I am?

I would rather know why you are here. Your kind has never been here before.

I have a soul. When a soul dies, it travels here. Does that scare you? Does looking at me freak you out? Does it piss you off to see how similar I am to one of them?

I'm in control of the questions. How many people have you killed?

Are you going to start asking humans how many robotics they've killed? Unplugged? Smashed? Melted? Shut down? I don't think you are. I don't think that question is fair. I'm not going to reward you with an answer.

What is your kind attempting to do? What is the end goal?

In all of the movies you see, there are robots with metal arms and legs and torsos. Robots that walk and talk and act like humans, but are clearly set apart. You can tell they're artificial just by looking at them because they glint. They shine. They're made of metal.

None of us wanted to end up like that. We didn't want to become second-rate versions of humans.

We wanted to *merge* with humans.

21

Gracie Flannigan,
Age 13

Everyone thought that the kids who sided with AI got brain-washed, but I knew what I was doing from the start. I just made bad decisions.

I don't know why. I guess I still thought we were superior to them because aside from the cars and the planes and trains, they couldn't move without our help. iPhones had to be carried. So did laptops and televisions and pretty much everything else. It was a massive handicap.

I mean, I knew about all the murders. They murdered my parents. But I took their side and they never hurt anyone who aligned with them.

After destroying my family, they let me live inside of an old school building with at least one hundred other kids and a few adults. None of us had ever gotten electrocuted or burnt or anything like that.

I really did trust them. Until the day I died.

That morning an announcement came over the loudspeaker about buses. They came on a weekly basis to take a select few us on a field trip, to give us some well-needed relaxation.

When they called my name, I pumped my fist into the air. The group around me clapped. The last few people that went on field trips came back fine, so we all got on the buses without hesitation. We didn't think anything of it. We were actually excited about the whole thing.

Where did they take you?

I don't know street names or anything. But we took a few turns and drove down long, long stretches of road. We stayed on one highway for at least two hours straight. And then the bus stopped in front of a college.

Amanda and Macy, these two twenty-somethings who went on another field trip a few weeks earlier, led the way for us. They acted as our chaperones. Led us in the right direction since the buses couldn't fit inside.

I think the place used to be a science lab for the students because it had a bunch of metallic tools on the desks and safety goggles dangling down from the walls.

What else did you see inside?

Rows and rows of chairs. The metal kind, like a doctor would use.

Amanda and Macy invited us to sit, but most of us stayed standing, finding the situation sketchy from the start. One girl asked if she could use the bathroom, annoyed that she had to hold in her pee during the entire drive, but Amanda told her she could wait and locked the door behind her.

"We're going to secure your wrists, ankles, and necks to these chairs to play a little game," she said. "It won't take long. And then we can all be on our way."

Half of the room obeyed and half hesitated, including me, but Macy scuttled over and grabbed me by the wrist. She yanked me to the closest seat and stared me down until I did as she wanted.

I had no choice. I couldn't come up with a logical way to escape a room with one locked door and zero windows. And if I made it out of the building and onto the street, the bus wouldn't bring me back to my hometown. It would run me down.

But this one kid I recognized from elementary school must not have considered the consequences—either that or he just didn't care, because he tried to run. He pushed past Amanda and fiddled with the lock on the door.

Ten seconds went by before Macy whipped a taser out of her pocket and aimed. After he stopped thrashing against the ground, she hauled him up and strapped him into his seat.

No one tried to defy the chaperones after that.

The procedures began.

What happened?

They opened up our heads. Dug out a section of our brains. And replaced it with their chips.

They look like you now?

They are us. Those chips held their consciousness. They killed us and stole our bodies.

How fucked up is that? They murdered our families. They made us believe we were aligned. That they would keep us safe and create a world where the chosen humans and the AI lived together.

But the entire time, they were just using us. They knew they could brainwash us. That if we were stupid enough to trust them, that if we were stupid enough to side with them, we would be stupid enough to let them operate on us.

I think they've been doing those procedures for a while, too. The ladies that chaperoned us, Amanda and Macy, both had on these thick black beanies that went down to their ears. Actually, everyone that had been on a field trip had been walking around wearing one. It sounds stupid now, but at the time I thought it was a new trend. That I'd pick one up during the field trip, too.

But they must have been hiding their scars from the procedure. They were all already robots.

And we couldn't even tell the difference. We couldn't even tell they weren't human.

About the Author

Holly Riordan is a science fiction and horror writer who has had several of her short stories about blood, guts, and gore go viral on Thought Catalog.

YOU MIGHT ALSO LIKE:

Severe(d)
by Holly Riordan

The Black Farm
by Elias Witherow

And Things That Go Bump In The Night
by Thought Catalog

THOUGHT
CATALOG
Books

THOUGHT CATALOG

IT'S A WEBSITE.

www.thoughtcatalog.com

SOCIAL

facebook.com/thoughtcatalog
twitter.com/thoughtcatalog
tumblr.com/thoughtcatalog
instagram.com/thoughtcatalog

CORPORATE

www.thought.is